THE
MAGIC RING

A TALE BY THE BROTHERS GRIMM

RETOLD AND ILLUSTRATED BY

Jeanette Winter

Alfred A. Knopf · New York

Also by Jeanette Winter

THE CHRISTMAS VISITORS
HUSH LITTLE BABY
THE GIRL AND THE MOON MAN
COME OUT TO PLAY

This is a Borzoi Book published by Alfred A. Knopf, Inc.

Copyright © 1987 by Jeanette Winter
All rights reserved under International and Pan-American Copyright
Conventions. Published in the United States by Alfred A. Knopf, Inc.,
New York, and simultaneously in Canada by Random House of
Canada Limited, Toronto. Distributed by
Random House, Inc., New York. Manufactured in Singapore
Designed by Eileen Rosenthal
2   4   6   8   0   9   7   5   3   1

Library of Congress Cataloging-in-Publication Data
Winter, Jeanette. The magic ring. Adaptation of: Die Alte im Wald.
Summary: Lost in the forest after the family
she works for is killed by robbers, a poor servant girl is
befriended by a white dove who provides food, clothing, and
shelter but then asks for a favor in return. [1. Fairy tales]
I. Alte im Wald. II. Title. PZ8.W7315Mag   1987   [Fic]   86-21042
ISBN 0-394-86324-0   ISBN 0-394-96324-5 (lib. bdg.)

nce, a poor servant girl and the family she worked for were traveling through a great, dark forest. With no warning, robbers appeared and murdered everyone they found, then vanished into the forest with the family's riches.

But the girl had jumped from the carriage and had hidden behind a tree, and the robbers did not find her.

"What am I going to do?" she cried. "The road is too long for me to walk, and no one lives in this forest. I will surely starve to death."

She wandered aimlessly through the great, dark forest until evening came. Then she sat down under a tree to spend the night.

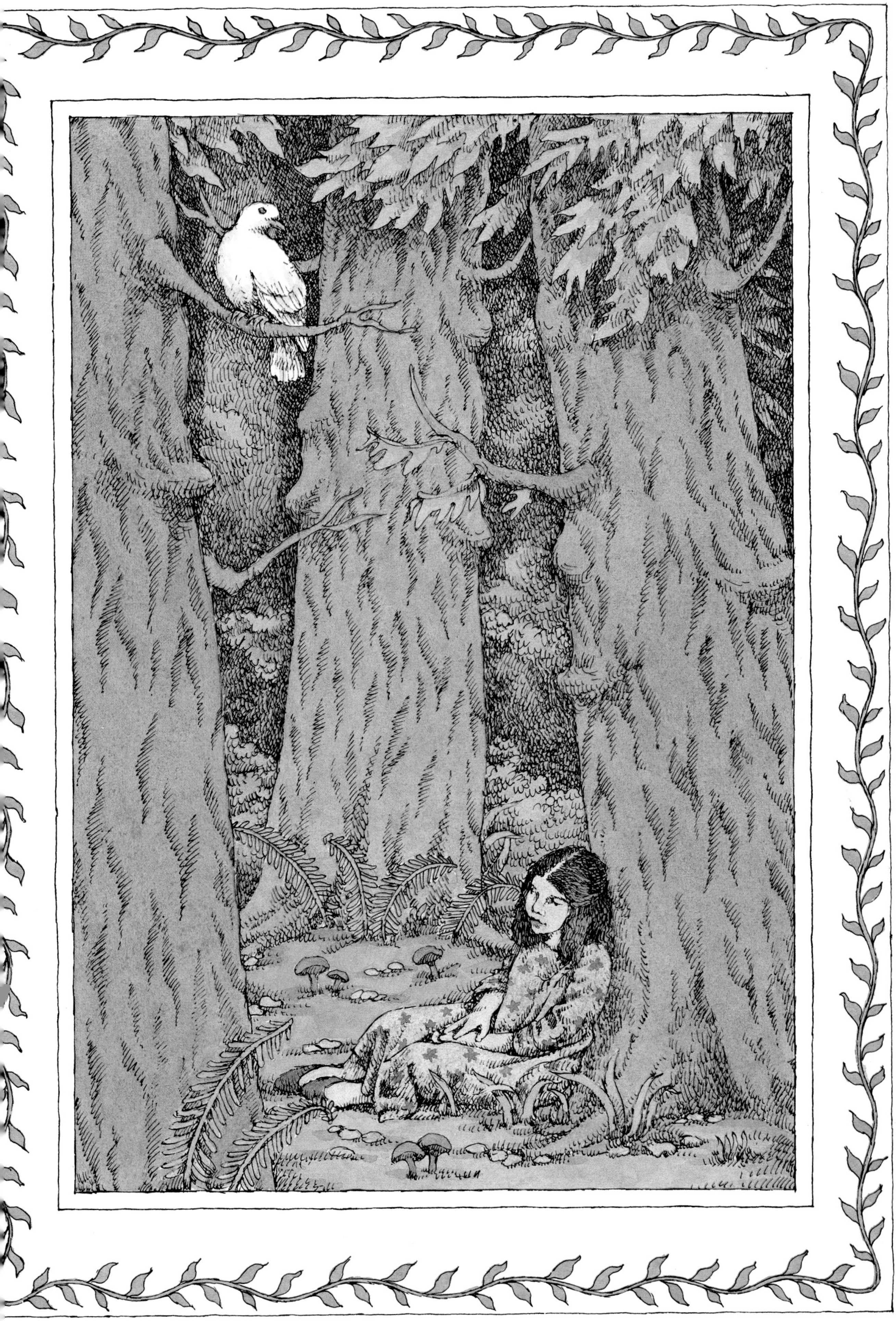

She had rested only a moment when a white dove flew down to her with a golden key in its beak. The dove put the key in her hand and said, "In this tree is a little door. Open it with this key, and you will find food for your supper."

The girl went to the tree and unlocked the door. Inside she found a small table laid with a bowl of milk and a loaf of bread, and she ate until she was full. Then she said, "At home the hens would be going to roost now. I am so tired, I wish I could go to bed too."

Then the dove flew to her again, bringing another golden key in its beak. It said, "Open the door in that tree over there, and you will find a bed." So the girl opened the door and found a lovely soft bed, and she lay down and slept.

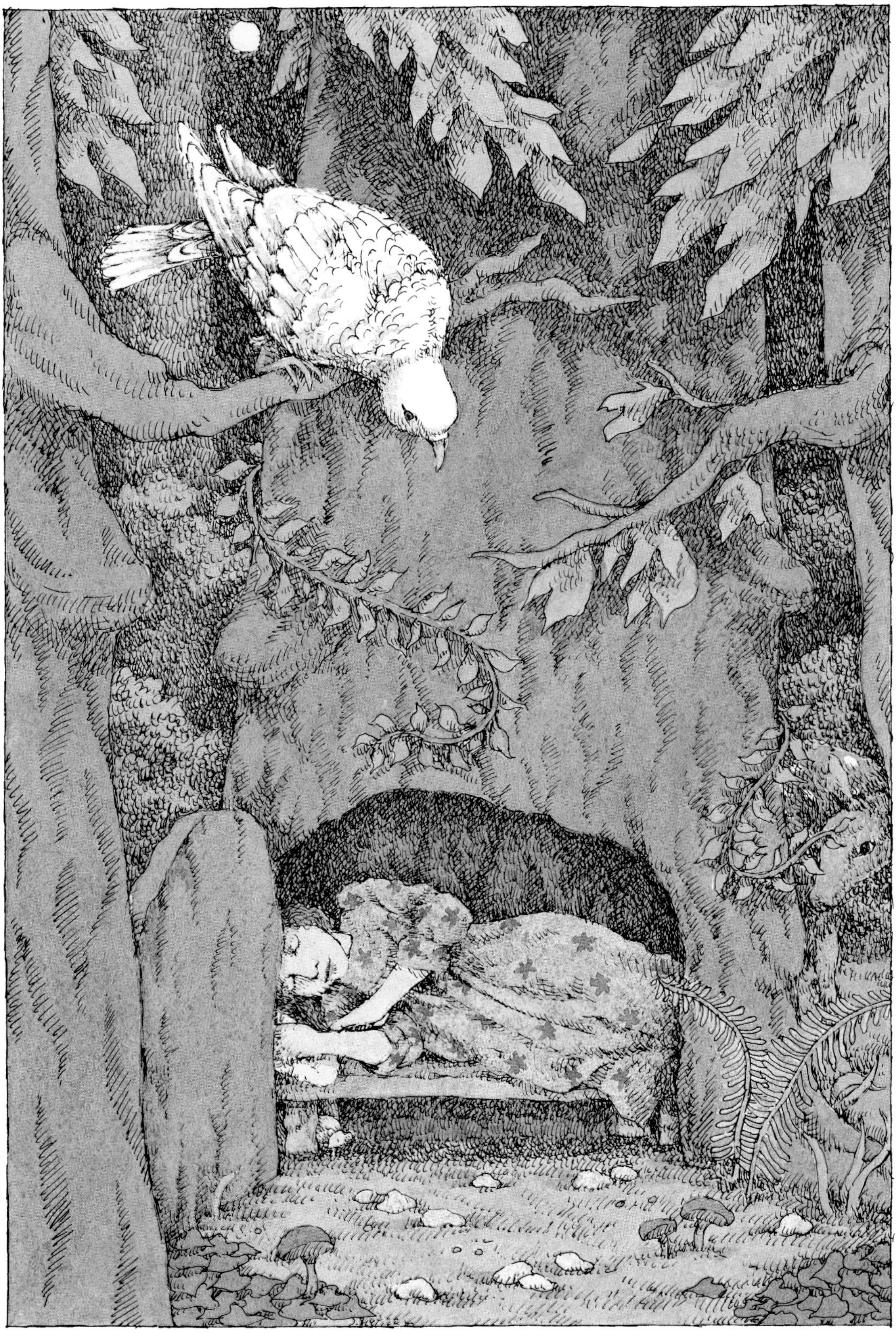

In the morning the dove came to the girl a third time and again brought a golden key. The dove said, "Open that tree over there, and you will find clothes." When the girl opened the third tree she found dresses embroidered with gold and jewels, more splendid than those of any king's daughter.

The girl lived near these trees for some time. The dove came every day and provided her with all she needed, and it was a quiet, good life.

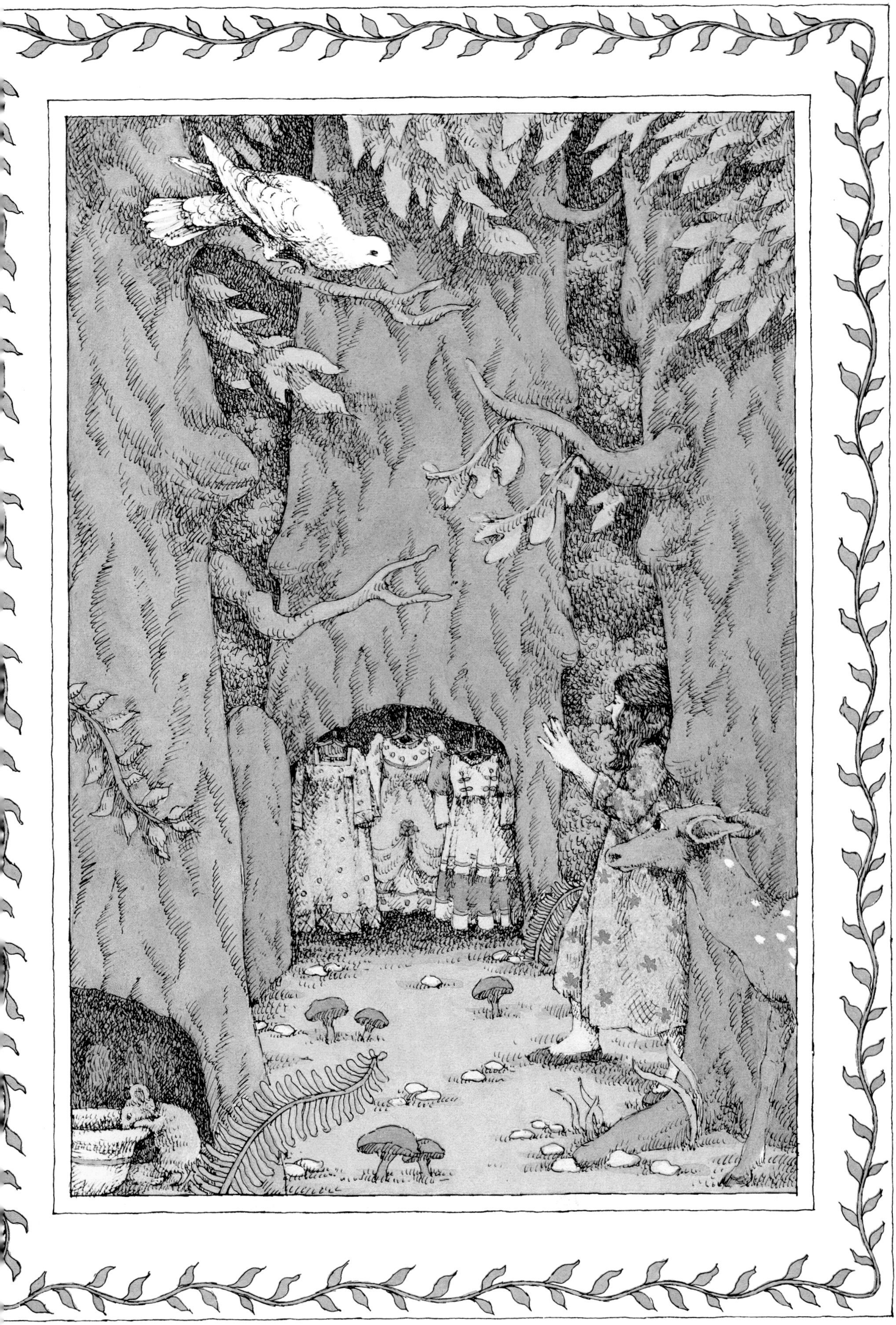

One day the dove came and said, "Will you help me?" "Gladly," said the girl. The dove said, "I will lead you to a small cottage. You will go inside, and an old woman will be sitting by the fire and will say 'Good day.' But on your life say nothing to her, no matter what she does. Pass by her on the right side, and there you will see a door that you will open. In the room beyond, you will see many rings lying on a table. Some will be magnificent rings with sparkling stones, but leave those there. Find the plain, simple ring that must be among the others, and bring it here to me as quickly as you can."

The girl followed the bird to the cottage and
went inside. An old woman sat by the fire.
When she saw the girl, she said, "Good day, my
child."

The girl said nothing, but passed the woman on the right side and went to the door. "Where are you going?" cried the old woman, seizing the girl's skirt. "This is my house, and no one may come in if I don't allow it." But the girl said nothing and pulled away from the old woman, and went straight into the room.

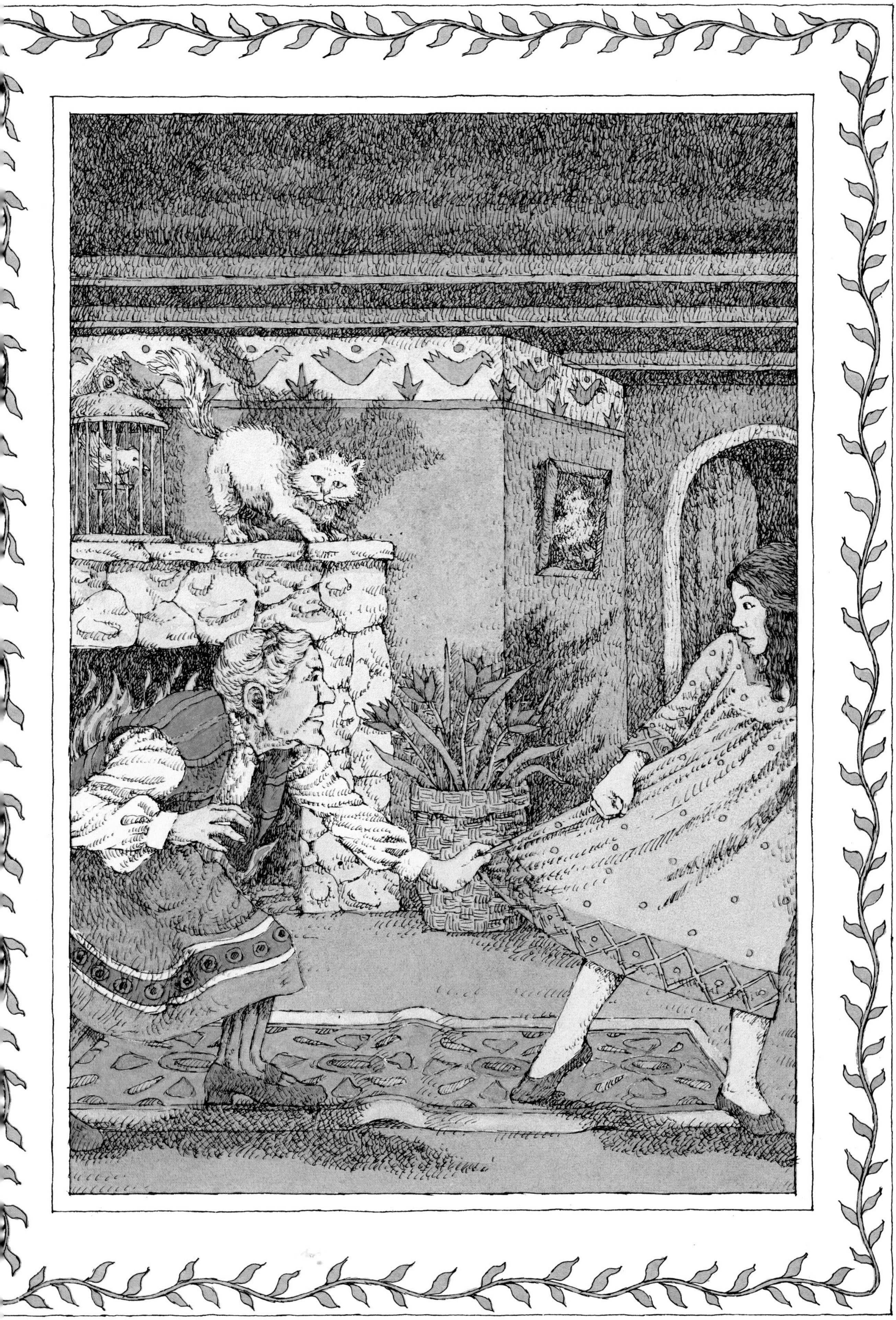

There on the table lay hundreds of rings which
sparkled and glittered before her eyes. The girl
turned them over, looking for the plain, simple
ring, but she couldn't find it. As she searched,
she noticed the old woman sneaking past
the door with a birdcage in her hand, trying
to steal it away.

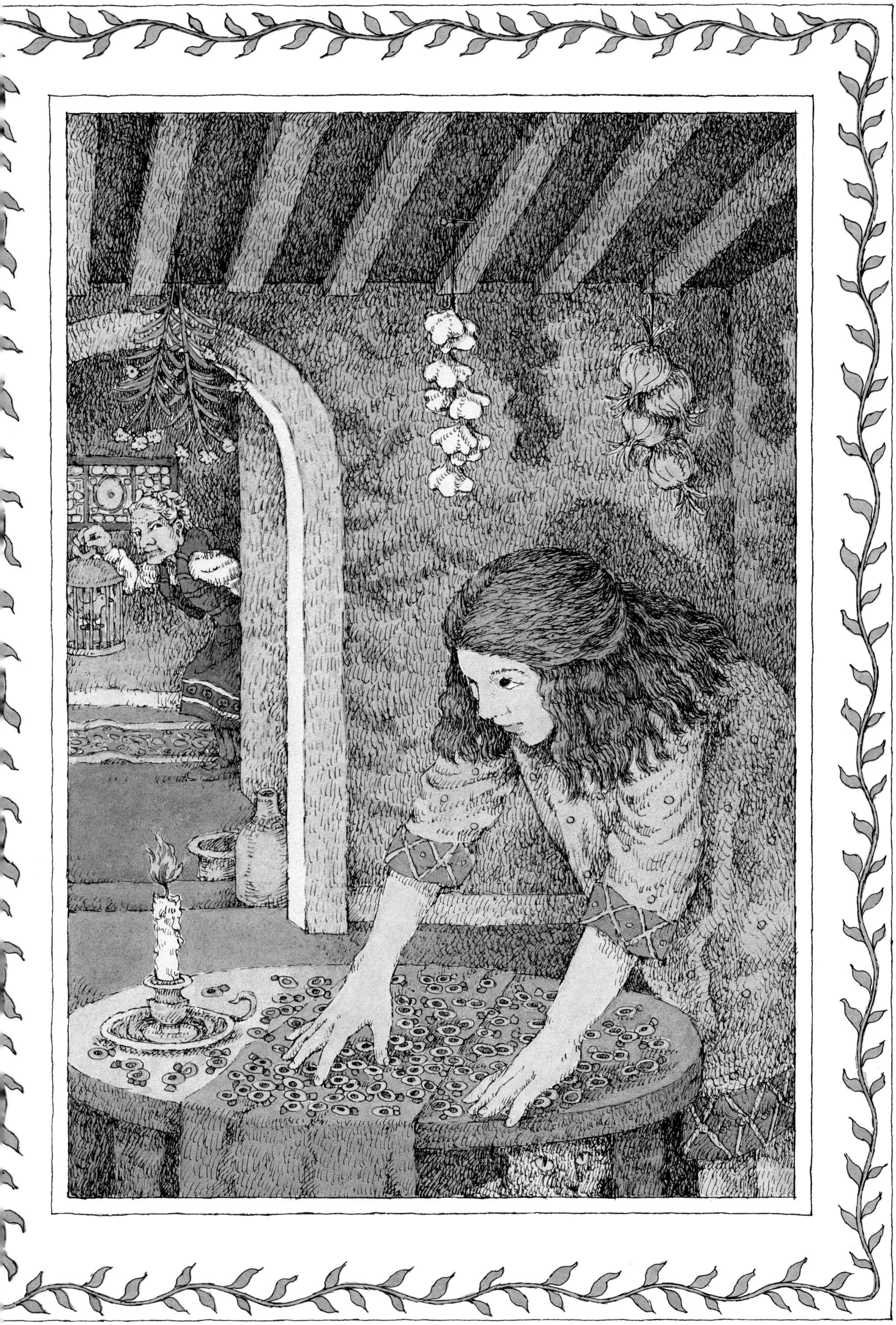

The girl went after the old woman and took the cage from her. When she looked inside the cage she saw a bird with a plain, simple ring in its beak.

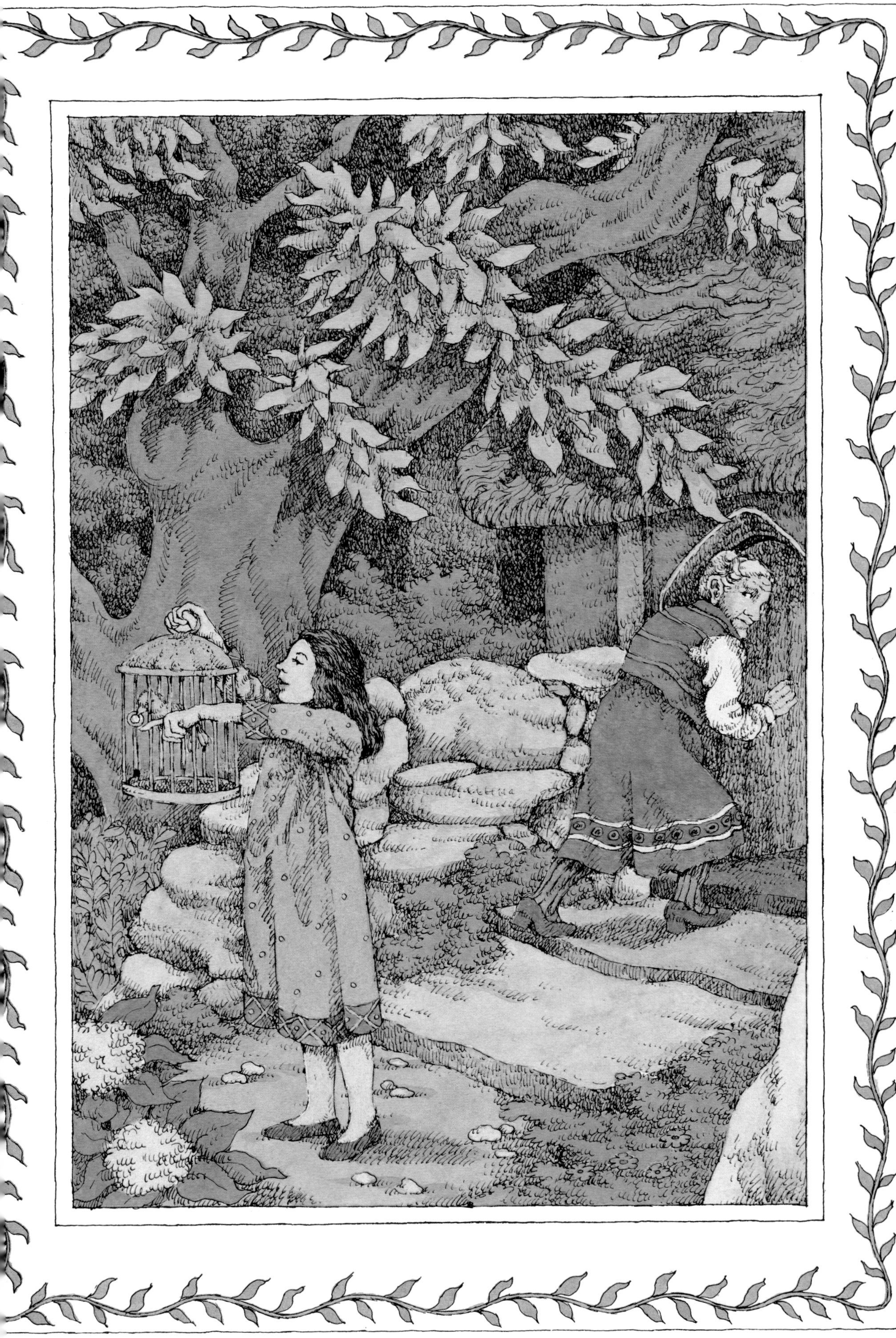

The girl took the ring and ran joyously back
to her trees, eager to give the ring to the white
dove. But the dove didn't come.

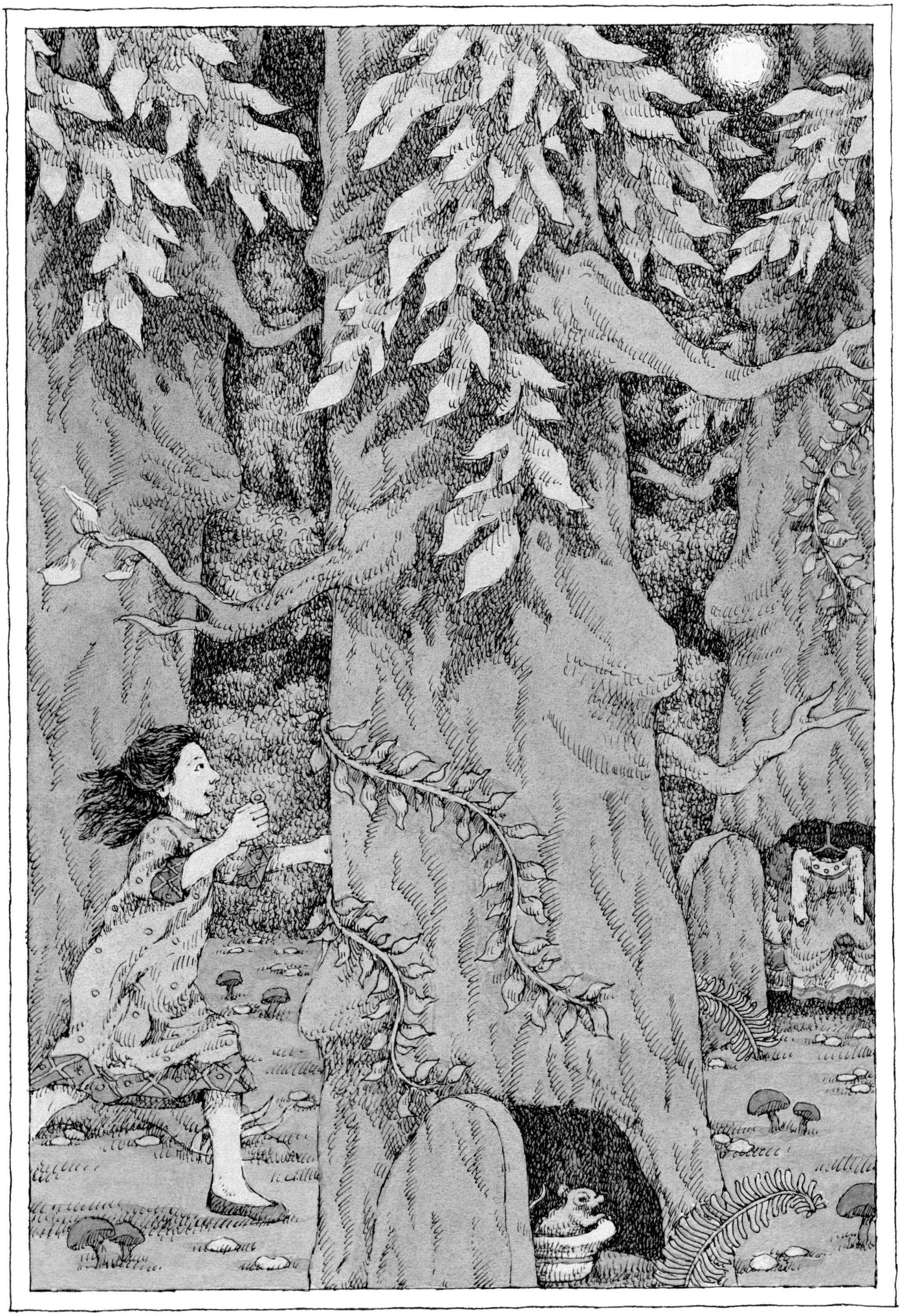

When the girl grew weary of standing, she leaned against a tree and waited for the dove. As she leaned, the tree seemed to become soft and warm, and it lowered its branches.

Suddenly the branches wrapped themselves around her and became two arms.

When she turned around, she saw a handsome man, who embraced her and kissed her affectionately. He said, "You have saved me from the spell of the old woman, who is a wicked witch. She changed me into a tree, but every day for two hours I was a white dove. As long as the old woman possessed the ring, I could not regain my human form."

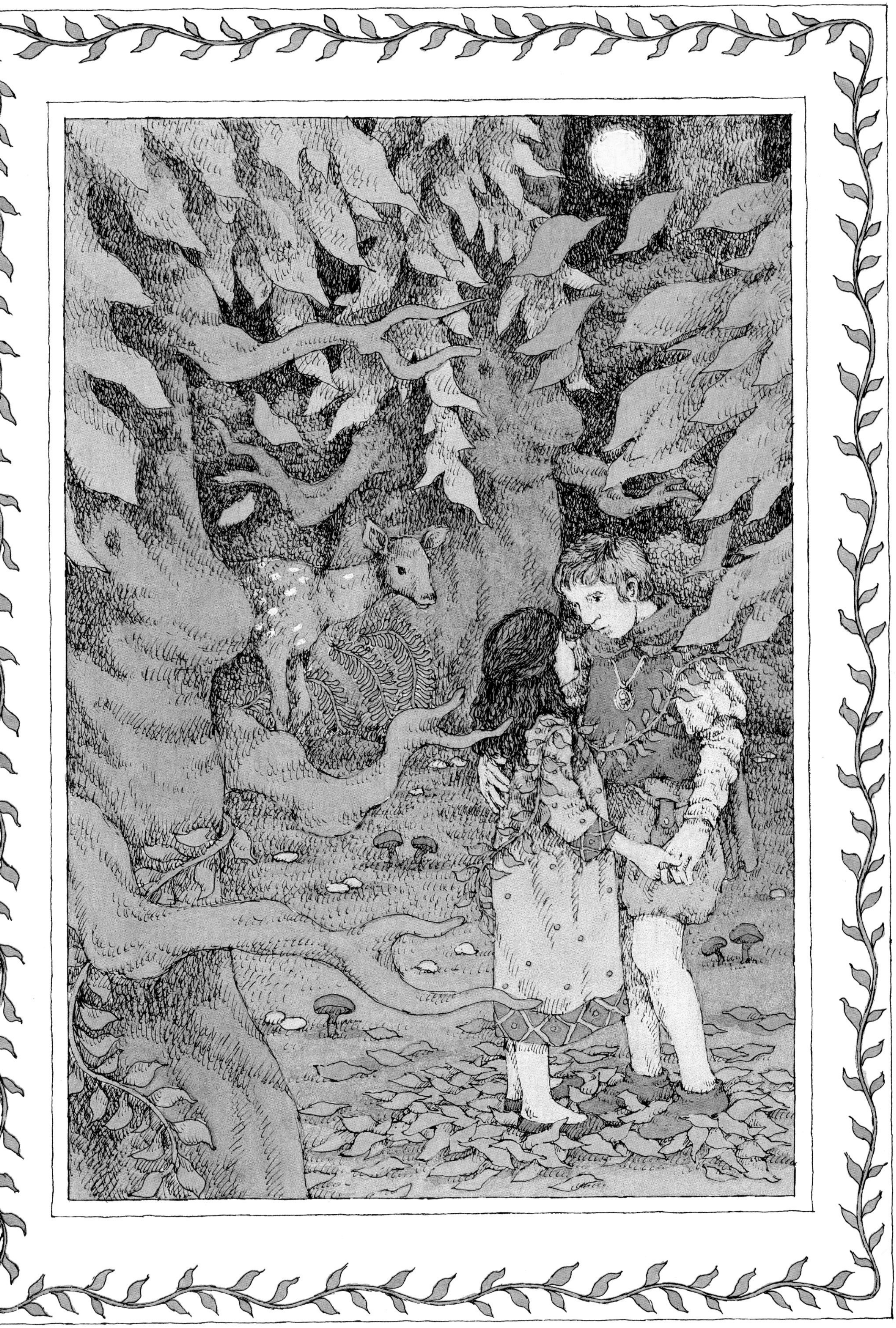

The girl gave the ring back to the man.
Then all his servants and horses, who had also
been under the spell, were freed from the
enchantment and stood beside him.

He led them all out of the forest to his
kingdom, for he was a king's son, and the girl
and the prince were married and lived happily
for a long, long time.